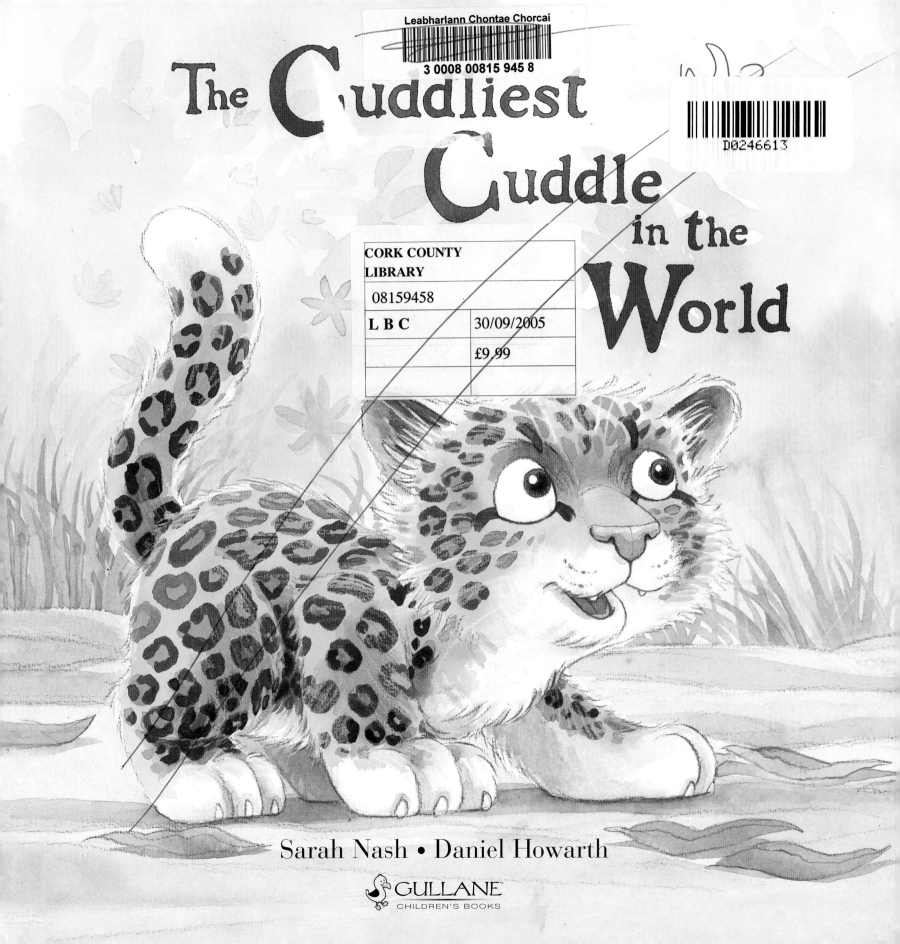

The Cuddliest Cuddle in the World

Sarah Nash • Daniel Howarth

GULLANE
CHILDREN'S BOOKS

Mummy's gone hunting. Leopard is left at home. Leopard is feeling lonely. He misses Mummy and he misses Mummy's cuddles.

"What's up, Spottychops?" says Bear.
"*No Mummy*," whispers Leopard sadly.
"How about a hug to cheer you up?" suggests Bear.

"AAAA... OUUCHHH... GET off," chokes Leopard.
"Your... hugs are muuchhh too tight!"

"Sssshall I give you a
ssssqueeze," hisses Python.

"*Stop it...*" giggles Leopard. "Your cuddles are far too tickly."

"Climb up here for a snuggle,"
calls Monkey.
"Help . . . let me goooo . . ."
screams Leopard. "Your cuddles
are much too whooshy!"

"Sha...ha...ha...ll I give you a
cu...hu...huddle?" chuckles Hyena.

"Yeuch!" splutters Leopard.
"Your cuddles are too licky."

"I will embrace you..."
smiles Crocodile.
"Ouch..." yelps Leopard.
"Your cuddles are
so snappy."

"Can I give you a huglet?" whispers Spider.
"Oh no . . ." smiles Leopard.
"Your cuddles are way too small."

"Oh dear," sighs Leopard, "I do miss Mummy."

"Listen up, Leopard,"
cries everyone,
"Mummy's back."

"Hello, little Leopard," says Mummy,
"did you miss me?"
"Mmmmm... and your cuddles..."
sighs Leopard.